"Awoooooooooh!"

Zoe and Lucy froze as a howling sound came from inside the Hall. Meep squeaked and leaped straight into Zoe's arms. Zoe felt quite scared, too! What was making that noise. . . ?

Look out for:

The Wild Wolf Pup

Amelia Cobb

Illustrated by **Sophy Williams**

nosy
crow

With special thanks to Natalie Doherty

For Lara and Isaac

First published in the UK in 2021 by Nosy Crow Ltd
The Crow's Nest, 14 Baden Place
Crosby Row, London SE1 1YW

www.nosycrow.com

ISBN: 978 085763 518 1

Nosy Crow and associated logos are trademarks and/or
registered trademarks of Nosy Crow Ltd

Printed and bound in Great Britain by Clays Ltd, Elcograf S.p.A.

Papers used by Nosy Crow are made from wood grown in sustainable forests.

Chapter One

A Special School Trip

Zoe Parker rushed excitedly towards
the Rescue Zoo gates, followed by her
teacher and the rest of the class.

"We're here!" she said happily.
"Welcome to the Rescue Zoo, everyone!"

"I still can't believe you actually *live*
here, Zoe," her friend Nicola exclaimed.

"You're so lucky."

"I know!" replied Jack, who was walking next to Nicola. "I can't imagine how cool it must be waking up every morning and seeing elephants and giraffes out of your bedroom window!"

Zoe grinned at her friends.

"It's so much fun!" she replied. "I've lived at the Rescue Zoo ever since I was a baby, and sometimes *I* still can't believe it!"

Zoe's Great-Uncle Horace was a world-famous explorer and animal expert, and he had started the zoo so that any lost, injured or endangered animals he came across on his travels would have a safe and caring home. Zoe's mum, Lucy, was the zoo vet, and Lucy and Zoe lived in a cosy cottage on the edge of the zoo.

Zoe adored animals more than anything,
and couldn't imagine living anywhere
else. As she and her friends reached
the gates, she felt like she might burst
with pride.

Zoe had been looking forward to this day for weeks. Halloween was coming up soon, and her class had been learning all about creatures like bats, beetles and spiders. Miss Hawkins had explained that lots of people thought these animals were scary or spooky, but that really there was nothing to be frightened of. Zoe had agreed – they were some of her favourite animals! Now everyone in the class loved them, and when Zoe had mentioned that the Rescue Zoo had a huge spider house, several types of snake *and* a big family of bats, Miss Hawkins had decided to organise a special class trip to the zoo!

Zoe's class had had normal lessons that morning, and after lunch they had set off together, walking through their town towards the zoo, carefully supervised by their teacher. Zoe couldn't wait to get to the Rescue Zoo – and neither could her friends! Lucy, Zoe's mum, was waiting for them at the entrance. "Hi, everyone!" she said as they walked inside. "You're right on time! I'm so glad you could all make it."

"Thank you for having us!" replied Miss Hawkins, smiling. "Where are we going to start?"

"I thought we'd go to the spider house first, which is over in that direction," said Lucy, pointing. "After that we'll go and see the bats, and, if there's time, the snakes right at the end. Zoe, why don't you lead the way?"

Zoe led her class proudly through the zoo, pointing out her favourite animals to Nicola and Jack as they walked along the path. "That's Leonard and Rory, our lions," she explained. "Well, Rory's a lion cub! And that's the panda enclosure. Chi Chi and Mei Mei are twin sisters, and they came all the way from China. They're really naughty, but so cute!"

Her friends peered into each enclosure, grinning broadly. But when they arrived at the spider house, Zoe spotted a grumpy-looking man waiting outside, wearing a spotless zoo uniform and hat, and holding a broom. "Oh no," she sighed. "Mr Pinch!"

"Who's that?" whispered Nicola. "Does he work here? He looks a bit cross!"

Zoe nodded. "He's the zoo manager," she whispered back. "He's always grumbling or groaning about something – especially mess. He hates it when anything's untidy!"

"I heard your class would be visiting the zoo today, Zoe," said Mr Pinch. "If you ask me, there is nothing that creates more mess at this zoo than school trips. Always dropping litter and  chewing gum and bits of packed lunch everywhere! If I see any mess, I'll know who was responsible." Mr Pinch narrowed his eyes at Zoe and her school friends, then muttered, "It's not as if I don't

already have enough to do without
sweeping up after you all. Being the zoo
manager is a *very* busy and important
job."

"Oh, you won't need to sweep up
after us," Miss Hawkins replied firmly.
"My class certainly won't be dropping
any litter or chewing gum, and they've
already had their packed lunches at
school."

"Hmmm. Even so, I still think I'd better
supervise," replied Mr Pinch, frowning.

Zoe's mum winked at Zoe and then
turned to Mr Pinch. "Oh, there's no need
for that, Percy," she said firmly. "I can
look after everyone!"

Lucy and Miss Hawkins ushered
everyone inside the spider house and
Mr Pinch shook his head, muttering

crossly to himself.

First of all, Lucy showed everyone a small enclosure with glass walls, full of moss, leaves and bits of wood. A delicate silver web had been spun between two branches, and a small black spider sat right in the middle of it. "This is an orb weaver spider," said Lucy. "Can anyone tell me what family spiders belong to?"

Straightaway, a boy called Louis put his hand up. "The arachnid family?" he said.

"Very good," said Lucy, nodding. "Lots of people think spiders are insects, but actually they're not – they're arachnids. Their bodies are made out of two sections, rather than three, and they have eight legs, not six."

"Look at that amazing web!" said Miss Hawkins.

"Spiders' webs are made from very strong silk," explained Lucy. "In fact, a strand of spider silk is five times stronger than a piece of steel the same size! And a spider produces lots of it. Some spiders spin themselves a brand-new web every day! Can you imagine building yourself a new house every day?"

Then she moved on to the next glass enclosure, and pointed out a big black spider with bright orange-red patches that was emerging out of a tunnel in the soil packed into the bottom of the enclosure.

"Now, here's a spider that *doesn't* live in a web – in fact, it lives in a burrow!" Lucy said.

"Wow!" breathed Jack. "What type of spider is it?"

"Rosie here is a red-knee tarantula!"

explained Lucy. "She might look a bit scary, but most tarantulas will never hurt a human. In fact, it's very rare to be bitten by a spider. Most spider bites happen when a person is frightening a spider, but if you're kind to them and leave them alone, they won't cause you any harm."

Zoe's friends rushed from spider to spider, taking pictures. Lucy even let Jack hold Rosie! Luckily, Mr Pinch hung back at the entrance, still glaring at the class as if he expected them to cause trouble at any moment. Zoe smiled to herself – she

knew he was secretly a little bit nervous
of spiders, and wouldn't want to get near
any of the enclosures!

Eventually Miss Hawkins clapped her
hands and said, "I think it's time we went
to see the bats, everyone. Make sure
you've got your bags and coats before we
move on."

As the class started to file out of the
spider house, Nicola tapped Zoe's arm.
"What's that?" she asked, pointing at a
big poster pinned up on the wall next to
the door. "The Rescue Zoo Spooktacular?
Is that a special Halloween event?"

Zoe nodded. "Usually the zoo closes
at six o'clock, but we're going to stay
open late on Halloween, so that visitors
can come and look around when
it's dark. We're going to decorate the

enclosures with carved pumpkins, and all the zookeepers are going to dress up as something spooky. There's a fancy dress competition for all the visitors too, with prizes. And we're going to bake Halloween cupcakes for everyone!"

"That sounds like so much fun!" said Nicola.

"Yes, it does!" added Miss Hawkins, who had overheard them. She looked thoughtful. "Actually, I noticed the poster as we were coming in, and now that I think about it, I have an idea…" She turned to Lucy and explained, "I've been teaching the class a special song, all about the so-called 'spooky' creatures they've been studying. We were going to perform it in assembly next week. Maybe it would be fun if they came and performed it at

13

the Halloween event, too?"

"That would be brilliant!" said Nicola immediately, her eyes wide. Zoe smiled. Her friend Nicola was really good at singing and even sang in the school choir.

Lucy was nodding enthusiastically. "That's a wonderful idea," she said. "We'll be setting up a little stage for the presentation of the fancy dress prize – maybe we could have a performance beforehand! The class could all wear their Halloween costumes and take part in the competition too. What do you think, Zoe?"

Zoe nodded and did her best to seem excited, but her tummy was suddenly feeling funny. Zoe didn't think *she* had a very good singing voice, and she felt nervous about singing in front of other people, even though she would be with her friend Nicola. Singing together in assembly wasn't too bad, because she knew all the other children at her school, so that wasn't as scary. But performing in front of lots of strangers would be very different. And the tickets for the Spooktacular night were almost sold out already. There was going to be a huge crowd – more than two hundred people! And now they were all going to watch her sing.

As Nicola skipped along, chatting excitedly about how much fun the performance was going to be, Zoe felt more and more worried. What was she going to do?

Chapter Two
Zoe's Costume Puzzle

Later that afternoon, when Miss Hawkins
had taken the rest of Zoe's class back to
school to be collected by their mums and
dads, Zoe and her mum decided to head
to the zoo café to have a hot chocolate.
As they walked there, Zoe thought that
the zoo was looking really colourful

and pretty, with red and orange leaves
fluttering down from the trees. She heard
a little squeak behind her, and looked
round. Something tiny, grey and furry
was scampering excitedly towards them!

"Meep!" called Zoe with a laugh. Meep
was a tiny grey mouse lemur, with a long
curling tail, bright golden eyes and a very
cheeky face. He was Zoe's best friend at
the zoo. Lucy smiled as Zoe bent down
to pick Meep up and give him a cuddle.
"Where were you earlier?" she whispered
to him so her mum couldn't hear. "I
thought you might come and see my
class!"

Zoe had a special secret, which nobody
else in the whole world knew, not even
her mum. She could talk to animals! It
made living at the Rescue Zoo extra

exciting, because every time Zoe heard
an animal roar, bark, grunt or hoot,
she understood exactly what they were
saying, and could speak back to them.

"I was going to come and see you,"
explained Meep. "But first I had a little
snooze. Then I felt hungry, so I had
a snack. There are so many treats in
the kitchen to nibble! I had a banana,
an apple, some nuts and some seeds."
Meep rubbed his belly
happily. "But then
I felt sleepy again,
so I thought
I'd better have
another nap!"

Zoe giggled.
Meep's two
favourite

things were sleeping and eating! Lucy had stopped to chat to the penguin keeper, so Zoe had a chance to reply. "That sounds like a nice day, Meep!" she said in a quiet voice, tickling his belly. "It's probably just as well you didn't come along anyway. Mr Pinch turned up and was grumpy with everyone. And you can never resist being extra naughty when he's around!"

Her mum finished her chat, and when they got to the café she bought them two mugs of hot chocolate with extra marshmallows. They went to sit in a cosy corner, and Zoe gave Meep one of her marshmallows, which he nibbled happily.

"Wasn't today fun, Zoe? It was lovely to have your whole class visit the zoo," Lucy said, taking a sip of her drink. "And I *loved* Miss Hawkins's idea about you all singing

at the Spooktacular! You'll be the stars of
the whole show!"

Zoe stirred her drink carefully and
avoided her mum's eyes. She didn't want
to admit that she was nervous about
singing in front of everyone. Luckily,
Lucy didn't seem to notice. "Oh, have you
decided what you'd like your Halloween
costume to be, love?" she asked. "We could
start working on it tonight!"

Zoe felt much more cheerful as she
thought about her costume. She loved
getting dressed up at Halloween! "I
haven't decided yet," she replied. "All I
know is that I want to dress up as an
animal! I went as a black cat last year
and a frog the year before, so I need a
new idea."

"How about a spider or a bat, since

that's what your class has been learning about?" suggested her mum.

"I think half of my class are already planning to come as spiders or bats!" Zoe explained.

Lucy nodded. "Hmm, yes, you want to go as something a bit different. Well, we'll think of something, Zoe! Why don't you and Meep go for a walk around the zoo and see if you get any inspiration?"

Zoe smiled. "That's a great idea."

When they'd finished their hot chocolates, Lucy went to the zoo hospital to check on a poorly meerkat. Zoe and Meep set off in the other direction. Meep ran up her arm and perched on her shoulder. "Who shall we visit first, Zoe?" he asked.

"Let's see…" Zoe looked around. "Well,

down this path are the crocodiles, the
zebras and the seals. A crocodile would be
a fun costume! Maybe I could wear my
green jumper, and make a special mask
with lots of sharp teeth."

"Yes! Or a zebra would be good too,"
added Meep. "You've got your stripy
black and white pyjamas, so you could
wear those. And then you'd just need a
tail and some ears."

"I wonder what Star thinks?" said Zoe.
They were just outside the seal enclosure,
where one of Zoe's favourite animals
lived: Star, the seal pup. "Let's go and ask
her."

Meep chirped eagerly. Gentle Star
was one of Meep's favourite animal
friends too!

Zoe reached for the necklace she was

wearing around her neck, and found the
little silver charm in the shape of a paw
print that dangled from it. She held the
charm against a panel in the gate, and
with a quiet click the gate swung open
for her. Zoe tucked the necklace back
under her jumper and smiled. It wasn't an
ordinary piece of jewellery, of course, even
though it looked like one. Great-Uncle
Horace had had it made especially for
Zoe, and given it to her for her birthday.
The charm opened every gate and door
in the whole zoo, so she could visit any
animal, whenever she wanted!

Star's enclosure was a pool of deep-blue
icy water, with a circle of smooth rocks
around it where Zoe sometimes sat to
watch Star and the other seals swimming.
Today Star was practising her somersaults

in the water, but as soon as she saw Zoe she gave an excited squeal and flopped straight out of the pool, shaking the water from her fluffy white coat.

"Hi, Star!" Zoe called, waving. "Wow, those backflips looked great!" She patted the seal on her fuzzy head. "Listen, I'm trying to think of a good Halloween costume, and I can't pick one! Do you have any ideas?"

Star suddenly looked very worried, and gave a nervous squeak. Zoe chuckled and bent down to pick up the little seal. "No, Star. Halloween isn't *really* spooky!" she reassured her. "Some of the zookeepers dress up as spooky things, like ghosts and witches, but it's not real. It's fun! In fact, it's one of my favourite days of the whole year."

24

Star didn't look too sure, and gave another little squeal. Zoe cuddled her close. "Oh dear! I think some of the other animals have been teasing you, Star," she said. "The Rescue Zoo is definitely NOT all creepy on Halloween! I've lived here for a long time and I've never seen anything scary at all. Except maybe Leonard the lion when he's in a grumpy mood!"

"Halloween is exciting, Star!"
added Meep, nodding his little head
enthusiastically. "The zoo is full of
balloons and other decorations, and there
are lots of treats to eat!"

Zoe hid a smile. Every year, Meep
also got frightened when *he* saw
people dressed up in spooky Halloween
costumes! Zoe always had to explain to
him that they weren't *really* witches or
skeletons – they were just normal people,
in costumes!

Eventually, Star seemed reassured. But
the little seal didn't have any costume
ideas for Zoe. Soon Lorna, the seal keeper,
arrived with a bucket of shiny fish for
their dinner, so Zoe and Meep waved
goodbye and headed back out on to the
path again.

Zoe sighed as they walked on. "Let's see. A tiger? A tortoise? A porcupine? There are just too many animals to choose from! I wish Great-Uncle Horace were here. I bet he'd have some good ideas," she said.

"Me too!" chattered Meep.

Great-Uncle Horace had been travelling around North America for over a month now. The last postcard he'd sent had said, *Helping a grizzly bear with toothache. Home soon!* Zoe couldn't wait to see him again – not just because she missed him, but also because Great-Uncle Horace often brought a new animal back to the Rescue Zoo when he came home!

"I wonder what he'll bring back next, Meep?" Zoe pondered out loud to her friend. She couldn't wait to find out!

At the end of school the next day, Zoe's class were still buzzing with excitement about their trip to the Rescue Zoo – and they were even more excited once Miss Hawkins had told them all that they'd be going back to the zoo on Halloween, to perform at the Spooktacular event!

"We should practise our song as much as we can until then, so we're really good!" said Sareeta, a girl in Zoe's class, as they all packed up their bags and started to walk out to the playground to meet their parents.

"Let's start now!" said her friend Jenna. She took a deep breath and sang the first line. "*Spiders and slugs, creeping on the wall...*"

Sareeta and Nicola joined in too.

"They're called creepy-crawlies but they're not so creepy after all…"

Nicola smiled at Zoe. "Come on, Zoe, you sing too! The next line is the one about bats and snakes, remember?"

But Zoe couldn't! As her friends looked at her, her mouth suddenly felt dry and her face went hot. All the words of the song were muddled up in her head. "Err – I can't sing today. My – err – my throat's feeling a bit sore. Sorry," she said quickly, rushing off to where her mum was waiting.

All the way home, Zoe worried about the Spooktacular. What if she froze like that when they were meant to sing their song on the night? Would everyone notice? *I could pretend to feel poorly so I don't have to sing,* she thought. *But then Mum will make me stay in bed and I'll miss the rest of the Spooktacular as well!*

When they got back to the Rescue Zoo, Meep was waiting for them at the gates. Zoe was about to head straight for the cottage, but Lucy said, "I need to go over to Higgins Hall to check on a pelican. Do you want to come along?"

Zoe said yes straightaway. A visit to Higgins Hall always made her feel better! It was the huge old manor house that sat on a hill overlooking the zoo, and it had belonged to Great-Uncle Horace's family for over a hundred years. It had once been very grand, but when Great-Uncle Horace had created the Rescue Zoo, he'd decided to turn almost all of its rooms into homes for different animals. He had just kept one attic room for himself and Kiki, his hyacinth macaw, to live in when they were at home.

But as they got closer to the Hall, Zoe noticed something odd. "What's that?" she said, frowning. There was a strange flickering orange light in one of the windows of Higgins Hall, and as they got closer she realised it was a Halloween pumpkin wearing a spooky grin. "Mum, did you put that pumpkin there?"

Lucy frowned. "No, I didn't. How

strange," she said. "And look – there
are cobwebs all over the front door!
They weren't there when I walked past
earlier—"

"*Awoooooooooh!*"

Zoe and Lucy froze as a howling
sound came from inside the Hall. Meep
squeaked in terror and leaped straight
into Zoe's arms. Zoe cuddled him, but she
felt quite scared too. What was making
that noise?

As Lucy reached out a hand to the
cobwebby door, they heard a deep,
booming voice cry, "Who's there?" – and
both Lucy and Zoe gasped as the door of
Higgins Hall burst open!

Chapter Three
Howling at Higgins Hall

Zoe stared for a moment at the figure standing in the doorway. Then she breathed a sigh of relief, her face broke into a grin and she rushed forward.

"Great-Uncle Horace!" she cried, jumping into his arms to give him a big hug. "It's you!"

"Wow, what a lovely surprise!" said Lucy. "We didn't know you were back!"

Great-Uncle Horace chuckled. He was wearing an orange jumper with a pumpkin on the front, and his untidy white hair looked even wilder than usual. His hyacinth macaw Kiki was perched on his shoulder, preening her beautiful blue feathers.

"I hope I didn't startle you!" he told them. "I just *love* Halloween, and I couldn't wait to start decorating the Hall. I got back to the Rescue Zoo about an hour ago from a wonderful trip to North America, where I'd got awfully used to taking taxis, so I did the same when I arrived back here! And the first thing I did when I got home was fetch the box of Halloween decorations down from the attic. And put my special jumper on, of course."

"So you put the pumpkin in the window, and the cobwebs on the door?" asked Zoe.

"Yes, that was me!" said Great-Uncle Horace, beaming. "Don't they look splendid?"

Zoe returned his smile, but she was still a little confused. "But what about that strange noise we could hear?" she asked. "Surely that wasn't you as well…?"

Great-Uncle Horace only smiled mysteriously in response, and then said, "All in good time, my dear! Now, why don't you come inside and see the rest of the decorations?"

They all stepped inside, and Zoe had to swallow her laughter as she looked

around the entrance hall. Great-Uncle
Horace had covered every single inch
of it in silvery cobwebs, plastic spiders,
rows and rows of bunting shaped
like skeletons, and
bunches of black
and orange
balloons.
"You don't
think it's
a little
bit over
the top,
do you?"
he asked
anxiously.

Zoe shook
her head. "It
looks brilliant!" she told him.

36

"Excellent!" said Great-Uncle Horace, beaming. "I'm so glad you like it. Oh, I saw a poster for the Spooktacular on my way to the Hall, and I must say, it sounds marvellous! I'm really looking forward to it. I have a fun idea for my costume too, but I think I'm going to keep it a secret for now!"

"Wait until you hear the best bit about the Spooktacular," Lucy told him. "Zoe and her class are going to sing! They've all been learning a special song at school, and they're going to do a concert for us. Everyone's very excited!"

"Really?" Great-Uncle Horace clapped his hands. "Well, now I'm looking forward to it even more! Was this your idea, Zoe?"

Zoe and Meep exchanged an anxious glance. Zoe didn't want to talk about the concert – especially not with Great-Uncle Horace. He and Zoe were very close, and Zoe knew he would guess that something was wrong. Quickly, she changed the subject. "Great-Uncle Horace – if you're back at the Rescue Zoo, does that mean you've brought a new animal home with you?" she asked. Then her eyes widened. "Is that what was making the noise?!"

Great-Uncle Horace smiled at her. "You're quite right, Zoe! I do have a new friend in tow!"

Just as he said that, there was another spooky howling noise from somewhere inside the house, and Lucy, Zoe and Meep jumped again!

"And there he is!" said Great-Uncle Horace. "Come on, I'll introduce you."

Great-Uncle Horace led them through

the hallway and along a corridor, while the howling sound grew louder and louder. Finally they stopped outside a door, and Zoe held her breath as Great-Uncle Horace pushed it open...

The howling suddenly stopped, and Zoe heard the pad of paws trotting towards them. Then a small furry face with huge dark eyes peered curiously around the door, and Zoe gasped.

"It's a wolf pup!"

Chapter Four
The Wild Wolf Pup

Zoe knelt down carefully and held out her hand, smiling as the pup gave it a cautious sniff, then a lick. "Is it a girl or a boy?" Zoe asked Great-Uncle Horace.

"A very boisterous little boy!" replied Great-Uncle Horace. "I found him in Alaska. He was separated from the rest of his pack by a fire in the forest where they lived. He's too small to look after himself, so the fire rescue team asked if I would bring him back to the Rescue Zoo, and of course, I said yes!"

"He wasn't hurt in the fire, I hope?" said Lucy with concern.

Great-Uncle Horace shook his head. "No, thank goodness. Just frightened at first – and he keeps howling, all day and all night, and I can't work out why. There are many different reasons why a wolf might howl, and I still need to get to the bottom of it. But other than that, he seems happy and friendly."

"He's beautiful," said Zoe, stroking the wolf pup's head. He was about the size of a small dog, with a dark-grey coat, pointed ears and a fluffy tail. His ears and

furry paws looked a little bit too big for
him, as if he needed to grow into them.
Zoe smiled at him and the pup gave a
bark, and then jumped up at her playfully,
trying to lick her face.

"I think he's decided he likes you, Zoe!"
laughed Lucy.

The pup rolled on to his back excitedly,
and Zoe giggled and leaned down to
tickle his soft fluffy belly. The little wolf
yapped happily, wriggling around and
wagging his tail. Then he jumped up,
nudged her arm with his head and
dashed off into the room, turning to see if
she was following him.

"He wants to play chase with me!" Zoe
realised, standing up and giggling. "He's
so funny!"

"I knew you'd like each other," said

Great-Uncle Horace, nodding happily.
"Perhaps you could think of a name for
him, Zoe? You're always good at that!"

Zoe chased the little pup around the
room until she was breathless. Even Meep
joined in, although he scampered quickly
up on to Zoe's shoulder when the wolf
pup turned around and started chasing
Meep, his little tail wagging excitedly!

"Where will he live, Great-Uncle Horace?" Zoe asked. The Rescue Zoo had a pack of Arctic wolves, but no grey wolves like the new pup.

"There's a spare enclosure next door to Luna and her family," Great-Uncle Horace explained, "so I sent a message to Ethan and some of the other keepers a week ago, and asked them to start getting it ready. I made sure they didn't tell you both, as I wanted it to be a surprise! We should be able to take the pup over there tonight. I'll call Ethan on my walkie-talkie and ask him to meet us there."

"I still need to check on that poorly pelican," said Lucy, "so I'll go and have a look at his foot, and then we'll take the pup to his new home."

"Oh yes, poor pelican! I'll join you,"

Great-Uncle Horace said. "He's in one of the rooms upstairs."

"Why don't I stay here with the wolf pup?" Zoe offered quickly. With her mum and Great-Uncle Horace out of the room, she'd be able to speak to the pup without anyone guessing her secret! She waited until their voices were a distant murmur and then turned back to the little wolf. "My name's Zoe!" she said in a friendly whisper. "And this is Meep, my best friend. What's your name?"

The wolf pup's tail started wagging even more eagerly when he realised Zoe could talk to him! He jumped up and put his front paws against her legs, and gave a happy bark.

"Shadow!" replied Zoe, grinning down at the little wolf. "That's a perfect name

for you, because of your lovely grey coat.
We're really glad you've
come to live at the
Rescue Zoo, Shadow.
Do you like it so far?"

Shadow gave another
eager bark. "Good! And
you're right, there are
lots of places
to explore
here,"
said Zoe,
smiling.
"And I
think you'll
like your lovely new enclosure too. It's
right next door to some other wolves, and
you'll get to see it tonight, as soon as—"

Suddenly Meep's ears pricked up.

"Zoe, someone's coming!" he told her urgently.

Zoe quickly stopped talking, just as her mum walked back into the room. "I forgot my medical bag," she explained, picking it up. She tilted her head to one side and paused before speaking again. "It's funny, Zoe – I heard you chatting to the pup just a moment ago and it sounded as if he was barking *back* at you. Almost as if you were talking to one another!"

Oh no! Zoe stared at her mum in horror. Had Lucy guessed her secret?

Chapter Five
Shadow's New Home

Before Zoe could think of an excuse, her mum chuckled.

"Silly me," she said, shaking her head. "Can you imagine – you and the wolf pup having a conversation!"

As she left again, Zoe let out a sigh of relief.

"That was close!" whispered Meep.

"I know!" admitted Zoe. "I'd better be more careful, Meep."

Once Lucy had given the pelican a check-up and some more medicine, they were ready to take the pup to the new grey wolf enclosure.

"Can I carry him?" Zoe asked hopefully.

"Of course!" replied Great-Uncle Horace, and helped her pick the little wolf up. Zoe kept one arm securely around his body so that he didn't fall, but made sure he could sit upright and see everything around him. This was going to be Shadow's first view of the zoo, and she knew he would want to get a good look!

As they walked through the zoo, lots of animals peered curiously over the

fences of their own enclosures to have
a look at the new arrival, and to call
out a friendly greeting. The pup was
very excited to see so many new faces,
and wriggled eagerly in Zoe's arms,
wagging his tail and letting out
little barks and louder,
longer howls. She
had to concentrate
to make sure she
didn't drop him!

"Oh, I've
thought of a
name for the wolf
pup," Zoe told her
mum and Great-
Uncle Horace,
smiling at Meep.
"Shadow!"

"Excellent!"
replied Great-
Uncle Horace.
"And a rather
mysterious, spooky-
sounding name too, which
I think suits a wolf perfectly.
Years ago, people were rather
frightened of wolves, you know, Zoe.
That's why they were often the wicked
character in fairy tales, like *Red Riding
Hood*." He shook his head.

"To look at this adorable little chap, it's hard to believe, isn't it? But sadly, grey wolves were almost hunted to extinction at one point."

"That's awful!" said Zoe, cuddling Shadow even tighter. How could anyone have been afraid of something as gorgeous as this?

"It's a pity Shadow won't have any other wolves to live with," said Lucy. "Wolves always form packs, and they're very social creatures. I'm worried that Shadow might find it very lonely here without any companions."

Great-Uncle Horace nodded. "Yes, I've been thinking the very same thing. Don't worry, my dear – I do have a plan. I can't say any more just yet though…"

Zoe and Lucy glanced at each other.

He was being very mysterious!

They soon arrived at the enclosure.
It was designed to look like a beautiful
sprawling wood, full of tall trees with
reddish-brown cones hanging from their
branches. "These are Sitka spruce trees,"
Great-Uncle Horace explained. "They're
the most important tree found in Alaska,
so hopefully they will help Shadow to feel
at home."

Zoe breathed in deeply as they stepped
inside. She thought it smelled amazing in
the enclosure – fresh and piney, like being
inside a real forest! Shadow seemed to like
it too. His ears were pricked up and he was
sniffing the air eagerly. Zoe placed him
gently on the ground and straightaway he
started dashing round, exploring.

Just then the wolf keeper, Ethan, arrived.

"Hello, everyone!" he called, waving. "I've been so looking forward to meeting this little fellow. Wow, look how cute he is! Does he have a name yet?"

"He's called Shadow," Zoe told him.

"Well, I hope Shadow likes his new home," said Ethan. "I brought him a little welcome present too." He held up a red bouncy ball, which he rolled gently across the ground towards Shadow. The little pup gave it a curious sniff, patted it with his paws – then he leaped on it excitedly, howling and barking! Meep, who had been sitting on the floor of the enclosure, had to scuttle quickly out of the way. He ran up Zoe's leg and up on to her shoulder as Shadow raced after the ball, leaping into the air and pouncing on it over and over again.

"Don't worry, Meep," Zoe whispered with a smile. "He's just playing!"

"I think he likes that game!" chuckled Great-Uncle Horace as they all watched Shadow playing boisterously.

In fact, Shadow liked the ball a little bit *too* much! He chased it around the enclosure, butting it with his head and snapping at it playfully with his white teeth, until there was a *pop*. Shadow had burst it! The little pup looked at the crumpled plastic, puzzled, and gave a sad little whine. Zoe quickly ran over to him and whispered, "Don't worry, Shadow – we'll get you another one."

Just then Lucy called, "Zoe? I think it's time we went home and had tea. Let's leave Shadow to get settled in. He's had a long day."

"Can't I stay a bit longer, Mum?" asked Zoe hopefully. She wasn't ready to leave Shadow yet, and before she did, she wanted to ask him if he really liked his new enclosure!'

Lucy smiled. "Five more minutes then. You can always come back to visit him after school tomorrow, remember."

While Lucy and Ethan chatted, Zoe crouched down next to Shadow. "What do you think of your enclosure?" she whispered. "Do you like it?"

Shadow wagged his tail and gave a happy yap. The little pup loved his new home! "We're going to have lots of fun together!" Zoe told him, smiling. "Meep and I will come back to play tomorrow."

Zoe gave Shadow one last cuddle, said goodbye to Great-Uncle Horace and

Ethan, and then left the enclosure with her mum and Meep. As they walked down the path back to the cottage, they heard a howl coming from behind them.

"That's Shadow! He's howling again!" said Zoe. She listened carefully, trying to work out whether the noise sounded sad or frightened. "Do you think he's OK, Mum?" she asked anxiously.

"I think so, Zoe. He certainly *seemed* happy, didn't he?" said Lucy. "Remember, a wolf doesn't only howl because it's unhappy. Animals make noises for lots of different reasons. They might be trying to communicate with other animals. They might be hungry, or warning off enemies, or just feeling content! Sometimes I wish I could talk to animals, Zoe – it would be amazing to be able to ask them exactly what they're thinking."

Zoe and Meep exchanged a glance. *I can talk to animals!* thought Zoe. *As soon as I can speak to Shadow with no one else around, I'll ask why he's howling!*

Later that night, Zoe and Meep were in her bedroom and Zoe was getting ready for bed. She'd brushed her teeth, put on her giraffe-patterned pyjamas and went to switch off her bedroom light. As she walked past her desk, she glanced at the calendar pinned up on her noticeboard and sighed.

"What's wrong, Zoe?" chattered Meep.

"There are only two days left until the Halloween Spooktacular, Meep," she said. "And I still don't have a costume idea…"

Suddenly Zoe's eyes lit up. "Hang on.

Maybe I do! Meep,
I could dress up
as a wolf, like
Shadow!"

"That's a
great idea,"
Meep replied.
"Then
maybe next
year you can
go as a mouse lemur!"

They both giggled. "Maybe!" said Zoe.
"But for now I bet Shadow would love
it if I dressed up like him! We can ask
him when we go back to play again
tomorrow."

"I'm not sure I want to play with
Shadow, Zoe," admitted Meep. "I like him
a lot, but he is a bit wild! He popped his

new ball, and I nearly got squashed when he was chasing me earlier! I think I'm too little for games like that," he said, his eyes wide.

"Oh, Meep – Shadow's used to playing with the other wolves in his pack," Zoe reminded her little friend. "He might not know how to play gently. And he was extra excited today! I'm sure he'll settle down soon though."

"I hope so," chirped Meep.

Zoe scooped her little friend up for a cuddle. "Don't worry, Meep! We just need to be patient with Shadow," she told him. "Remember how strange and different things must be for him. He's probably feeling a little bit nervous about moving to a new home. Being nervous can make you act strangely sometimes."

"What do you mean?" asked Meep, puzzled.

Zoe thought. "Well, a new boy, Dan, started in my class last year. He moved here from a different school and he didn't know anybody, but instead of being friendly, he was really rude to everyone! But once he settled in and got to know everyone, he was really nice. He just acted like that because he was nervous." As she spoke, Zoe realised something else. "And being nervous about the Halloween concert has been making *me* feel a bit funny too!" she said. "Whenever I think about singing in front of the crowd, my tummy ties up in knots and my knees feel shaky." She sighed. "I just don't know how I'll be able to do it!"

"I think you'll be really good, Zoe!"

said Meep. "Maybe you just need a bit more practice. Why don't you have a go now? Pretend that I'm the audience!"

Zoe thought that was a good idea. She'd only be singing in front of Meep, after all – her best friend in the whole world! She took a deep breath and tried to sing the first line of the song. "*Spiders and slugs, creeping on the wall. . .*"

But even now, Zoe couldn't do it. Her throat felt dry and sore, and her voice sounded hoarse and scratchy. She stopped, shaking her head sadly. "I just keep picturing a huge crowd of people, all pointing at me and laughing," she said. "I know that must sound really silly, but I can't help it."

Meep leaped into Zoe's arms and gave her a cuddle. He nuzzled his head against her. "It will be OK, Zoe! We'll think of something!" he chirped helpfully.

Zoe smiled and nodded. But deep down, she wasn't sure.

Chapter Six
Some Exciting News

"Hi, Ethan!" called Zoe, waving as she slipped into the wolf enclosure. "We've come to play with Shadow, is that OK?"

Ethan waved back. "Of course, Zoe!"

It was the following day, and Zoe had rushed back from school as quickly as she could, desperate to visit Shadow again.

She had managed to persuade Meep to
come along too, even though her lemur
friend was still nervous about playing
with the wild little wolf. All the way
to the enclosure, they'd heard Shadow
howling noisily, just like yesterday. But
when they arrived and Shadow saw them
both, he started barking happily and
wagging his little tail. Zoe went straight
over to him and knelt down, and Shadow
gave her hand lots of excited licks.

Ethan said, "He looks very pleased to
see you! You know, he hasn't started to
calm down yet. I've hardly been able to
keep up with him today – I'm exhausted!
He's really keen to play-fight, like he
would with other wolves in his pack."
Ethan showed her a few scratches on his
hands and arms from where Shadow had

got overexcited. "I brought him a new
ball, but he chewed it up straightaway!"
he added with a tired smile, nodding at
a few shredded bits of blue plastic on the
ground.

As soon as Meep heard this, he leaped
straight on to Zoe's shoulder. "I'm staying
up here today!" the little lemur said
firmly. "What if Shadow thinks *I'm* a
bouncy ball too?"

"Don't be such a scaredy-lemur," Zoe
whispered back when Ethan disappeared
into a store cupboard to fetch something.
"Shadow won't hurt you!"

Ethan came back with a long, smooth
plastic sheet and a tray of ice cubes. "But
I have found something Shadow loves –
watch!" he told Zoe.

He spread the plastic sheet out on the

ground and shook the ice cubes into
the palm of his hand. Shadow watched,
his head cocked to one side and his tail
wagging. Then Ethan slid the ice cubes
along the piece of plastic – and with a
yelp of excitement Shadow pounced after
them! Zoe giggled as the funny little pup
chased the ice cubes around the plastic,
nudging them forward with his nose so
that they shot away from him, and then
sliding and skidding along behind them.

Finally, when they started to melt more, he crunched the cubes up noisily with his tiny teeth.

"That was so cute!" Zoe said, still laughing. "What other games have you been playing with him, Ethan?"

Ethan pointed to a black rubber bicycle tyre. It was full of holes and bite-marks. "I tried to teach Shadow how to fetch this tyre," he said, "but he was more interested in chewing it to pieces than bringing it back for me to roll again. Do you want to have a go, Zoe?"

Zoe took the tyre from Ethan and held it next to her. Shadow pricked his ears up expectantly, watching her. As soon as Zoe rolled the tyre along the ground, he raced after it, his tail wagging. When he caught up with it he grabbed it in his mouth.

Then he started shaking it from side to
side, making playful growling noises and
chewing even more holes through the
rubber.

"Shadow's already
bitten through three tyres
today," Ethan told Zoe. "Mr Pinch walked
past earlier and was really cross about
all the mess! I'll have to go shopping
for more toys tomorrow – although I
bet Shadow will chew straight through
whatever I give him to play with!"

"He really is pretty wild, isn't he?"
said Zoe.

Ethan nodded. "I think it might be to do with him being separated from his family," he said. "It must have been really difficult for him. He'll have been used to playing and wrestling with the other wolves in his pack."

"Well, I've got some exciting news about that!" said a voice from behind them.

Zoe and Ethan turned round just as Great-Uncle Horace stepped into the enclosure. "What do you mean?" asked Zoe.

Great-Uncle Horace beamed. "We've found the rest of Shadow's pack!" he explained. "They ran away from the fire that destroyed their home and took shelter several miles away. They have a few minor injuries, but with treatment they'll be fine."

"That's really good news!" exclaimed
Ethan.

"Yes, and now that they've been located,
Shadow should be reunited with them,"
added Great-Uncle Horace. "And because
their territory was destroyed by fire, the
best thing seems to be for them all to
come to live at the Rescue Zoo."

"That's what you were being so
mysterious about the other day, when
you said you had a plan but you couldn't
tell us what it was!" Zoe realised.

Great-Uncle Horace nodded. "I didn't
want to get anyone's hopes up, my dear,"
he explained. "I knew the fire rescue team
in Alaska were searching for the pack,
but we couldn't be sure they would find
them."

Zoe looked carefully at Great-Uncle Horace. Even though he was telling them such a good piece of news, she realised that he was frowning anxiously. "What's wrong, Great-Uncle Horace?" she asked. "You look worried."

Great-Uncle Horace sighed. "Well, I'm afraid there's a bit of a problem too," he said. "You see, even though there were only four other wolves in the pack – Shadow's mother, an older brother and two babies – and we have plenty of space for them to live here at the zoo, flying them over will be very expensive. We're going to have to find some extra money from somewhere if we're going to be able to reunite the pack with Shadow and treat them for their injuries here."

As Great-Uncle Horace and Ethan

talked about how they could raise the money to fly Shadow's pack over to the zoo, Zoe felt a little nudge against her leg and looked down. Shadow had overheard what Great-Uncle Horace had said, and wanted to know what was going on!

Zoe bent down and, checking that Great-Uncle Horace and Ethan were too busy chatting to overhear, whispered to Shadow, "Your pack has been found, and they're all OK!"

Shadow's big dark eyes suddenly widened! He let out a happy, excited bark and bounded around in circles, wagging his tail so fast it was a blur. Then he raced back over to Zoe and yapped hopefully.

"Well, Great-Uncle Horace and everybody else really *want* them to come and live here with you," replied Zoe

quietly, deciding she should be honest
with Shadow about the tricky situation.
"But there is a little bit of a problem at
the moment. They're very far away, you
see—"

Meep suddenly squeaked a warning
as Great-Uncle Horace and Ethan
turned back round, so Zoe couldn't finish
explaining to Shadow. The little wolf
pup was suddenly looking very worried,
yapping more and more questions, and
then he began to howl again. But in front
of Great-Uncle Horace and Ethan, Zoe
knew she couldn't keep talking to him
and risk giving her secret away.

Very soon, it was time for her to head
home for tea, and there was no other
opportunity for her to speak to Shadow
alone. As she and Meep walked back to

the cottage, they heard even more howls coming from his enclosure, and this time Zoe could tell the wolf was feeling very anxious – and she was too.

Despite worrying about Shadow, Zoe felt a little better when Lucy helped her put the finishing touches to her wolf costume later that evening.

"There! Just another couple of stitches to keep this furry ear on nice and tight, and I think we're almost finished," said Lucy. "What do you think, sweetheart? Sweetheart?"

Zoe looked up, realising she'd been thinking about Shadow and his pack. "Oh, sorry, Mum. I love it," said Zoe, reaching over to hold the costume up in front of her. "It's going to look brilliant."

Zoe's mum looked at her carefully. "You seemed a little bit down while we were having tea. Is everything all right? Are you worrying about how we're going to find the money to bring Shadow's family over to the zoo?"

"Yes," admitted Zoe. "I wish I could think of a good way to raise lots of money. I just don't know what to do!"

Lucy nodded. "I know, Zoe. I wish I could think of something too."

"I've got my birthday money in my piggy bank," offered Zoe. "But it's not very much."

Lucy smiled at her. "That's very generous of you, Zoe. And every penny helps, when you add them up! I bet there would be lots of people who'd give a little bit of money to help bring the rest of Shadow's pack over – if they only knew about their situation and the help they need." She sighed thoughtfully as she sewed the last few stitches into Zoe's costume. "What we really need is to gather lots of people together in one place, all at once, so that we can tell them the story of Shadow and his family."

Zoe looked at her mum. "Wait! I

think I've got an idea. The concert at
the Spooktacular! What if we make it a
charity performance? We could explain
about Shadow before we sing our song.
Then, if people like our singing, and want
to help Shadow and his pack, they could
put some money in a bucket, and we can
put it all towards paying for Shadow's
family to join him here at the zoo, where
we can look after them all properly!"

Lucy beamed at Zoe. "That is a
brilliant idea," she said. "I think Great-
Uncle Horace will love it."

Zoe nodded. "Now I just need to
ask one more person," she said. "Miss
Hawkins!"

Chapter Seven
The Spooktacular Begins!

"Mum, Mum!" cried Zoe as she ran out into the school playground to meet Lucy. "Miss Hawkins said yes!"

"That's fantastic news, Zoe," Lucy replied, smiling. "Well done!"

As soon as Zoe had arrived at school that morning, she'd gone straight up to

Miss Hawkins and explained her idea. She'd even brought in a photo of Shadow that Lucy had taken on her phone and printed out for Zoe.

Miss Hawkins had agreed immediately. "I think that's a wonderful suggestion," she told Zoe. "Let's tell the rest of the class after I've taken the register." She'd even asked Zoe if she could keep the picture of Shadow! "I'll pin it up on the class noticeboard, so everyone can see the little fellow we're trying to help," she'd explained.

All day, Zoe had been desperate for the last bell to ring. When it did, Miss Hawkins clapped her hands and called, "All right, everybody, time to go home. Remember, your parents or guardians need to bring you to the Rescue Zoo by seven o'clock tonight, and we'll be singing at half past seven. I can't wait to see your costumes! See you all there!"

Zoe had been so excited about her idea to help Shadow, she'd almost managed to forget about singing at the Spooktacular that evening. But as she walked through the playground with her mum, she heard some of the other children from her class practising the words, and she felt a familiar nervous feeling in her tummy. *Just think about Shadow,* she told herself firmly. *This is for Shadow!*

When she and Lucy arrived at the gates of the Rescue Zoo, Zoe had a surprise. Two huge bunches of orange and black balloons had been tied to the gates, and a banner had been stretched along the top of the entrance, which read:

WELCOME TO THE RESCUE ZOO HALLOWEEN SPOOKTACULAR!

Enjoy our world-famous zoo and amazing animals after dark! Enter our fancy dress competition, hear our bat expert talk about these fascinating creatures, and come along to a special Halloween concert at 7.30pm

<u>All</u> money raised tonight will help us to fly a very special family of grey wolves to their new home at the Rescue Zoo!

Zoe looked up at her mum. "*All* money raised?" she repeated. "I thought just the donations we collect at our concert were going to help Shadow?"

Lucy smiled. "When I told Great-Uncle Horace your idea to help Shadow this morning, he liked it so much that he decided the whole Spooktacular would be to help Shadow," she explained. "All the money we raise from the ticket sales, from the raffle, from people buying toffee apples and hot dogs and candyfloss. Everything!"

Zoe couldn't believe it. In just one night, maybe the zoo would be able to raise all the money they needed to fly Shadow's pack over to join him! Then the little wolf pup wouldn't be alone any more.

"Zoe, hurry up! I want to see your costume!" squeaked Meep, hopping up and down excitedly.

"I'm almost ready!" replied Zoe. "Keep your eyes closed until I say, Meep, and no peeping!"

Zoe and Meep were in Zoe's bedroom. It was after tea, and almost time for the Spooktacular to begin! Meep was perched on the bed with his tiny paws covering his eyes, while Zoe pulled on her grey wolf costume: grey leggings, a fluffy grey jumper, and furry grey gloves and boots. Now she just had to add a woolly hat with furry ears attached, and colour her nose in black using an eyeliner pencil that her mum had let her borrow.

"OK, Meep – now you can open your eyes!" said Zoe.

Meep took his paws away. "Wow, Zoe!" he chirped, his eyes wide. "You really look like a wolf!"

Zoe giggled. "Thanks, Meep! I hope Shadow likes it. I can't wait to see what everyone else in my class looks like too, especially Jack and Nicola!"

"*Woooooooo!*"

Meep nearly fell off the bed in fright as a spooky moaning sound came from outside. "What is that, Zoe?" he squeaked, looking around nervously.

Zoe ran to the window and looked out.

"Oh, Meep, it's nothing to be worried about!" she laughed. "It's just some of the zookeepers. They've made a recording of scary Halloween sounds and they're going to play them over the zoo loudspeakers as all the guests arrive!"

"I'm not sure I like that idea," grumbled Meep.

Zoe giggled and scooped him up for a cuddle. "Meep, remember what we told Star the other day? Halloween isn't *really* scary. It's fun!"

Just then, there was a knock on Zoe's bedroom door, and a spooky green face with a pointy nose and wild black hair appeared! Meep gave another terrified squeak and hid his face against Zoe's jumper.

"Oh dear!" said Lucy, coming into the

room. "I think I might have frightened Meep. I suppose I do look quite scary! What do you think, Zoe?"

Zoe smiled. Lucy was wearing a long black dress, pointy black shoes, a wig of messy black curls and a tall black hat covered in silver cobwebs. She had covered her face with green face-paint and a fake green nose. "You make a great witch, Mum!" she said.

"And you make an excellent wolf!" replied Lucy. "I wonder what Great-Uncle Horace will dress up as? He still won't tell anyone!"

Another spooky noise came from outside. This time it was a wicked-sounding cackle.

"*Ahahahaha!*"

Lucy smiled. "I think everything's about

to start!" she said. "Are you ready to go, love?"

"Ready," said Zoe. "Everyone in my class is supposed to meet outside the café."

"Come on then – I'll walk you there," said Lucy. "I'll just fetch my broomstick!"

As Lucy, Zoe and Meep walked through the zoo, Zoe couldn't believe how busy it already was. The paths were bustling with crowds, all dressed up as witches and black cats, spiders and toads, skeletons and vampires.

Meep was still nervous, and snuggled down in Zoe's arms to begin with, but after some reassuring whispers from Zoe he started to look around, and as soon as he realised everyone was having lots of fun, he cheered up.

"They're just normal people in costumes, remember!" Zoe told him quietly.

Meep cheered up even more when Lucy gave them both a bag of Halloween treats to share. "There are jelly frogs and chocolate bats for you, Zoe, and lots of fruit and seeds for Meep," she explained.

"I've remembered that I like Halloween after all," Meep whispered to Zoe as he nibbled a treat, which made her giggle.

Everyone seemed to be enjoying the Spooktacular. There was a raffle set up outside the penguin enclosure, an apple-bobbing stall by the rhinos, and face-painting a little bit further along.

Zoe saw some of the zookeepers walking around with trays of hot apple juice in black and orange cups, and some others handing out biscuits in the shape of spiders and bats, and the special Halloween-themed cupcakes Zoe had made with her mum. Spooky orange pumpkins lined the path, lighting up the whole zoo, but Zoe thought it all felt very fun and friendly, rather than scary.

Even Mr Pinch seemed to be enjoying himself, despite having been so grumpy the other day about all the mess the Spooktacular would make. He was munching a toffee apple as he queued up to buy a raffle ticket. Zoe nudged Meep and pointed to the zoo manager.

"Look, Mr Pinch is actually having fun!" she whispered.

When they turned the corner and arrived at the café, Zoe saw that almost her whole class was already there. "Everyone looks brilliant!" she said. "Look, Mum – Miss Hawkins has dressed up as a witch too!"

Miss Hawkins wore a tall pointy hat like Lucy's, but hers was purple with gold stars, and instead of a broomstick she held a furry toy cat under her arm. "Hello!" she called. "I love your costumes. I think I recognise yours from the photograph you brought to school, Zoe. You've come as Shadow the wolf!"

Zoe grinned. "That's right!" she said. "I like your costume too, Miss Hawkins."

Jack and Nicola arrived together. Jack was dressed as a scary pirate, with a black eyepatch, a hook over his right hand and

scars drawn in red pen all over his face.
Nicola was a zombie ballerina, wearing
a pink tutu and ballet shoes, and lots of
spooky make-up.

"You two look amazing!" Zoe told
them.

"So do you! I can't wait to meet the
real Shadow," Nicola replied.

"Yes, can we go and meet him now?"
asked Jack hopefully.

"Not just yet!" said Miss Hawkins,
overhearing them. "First we're all going to
take part in the costume parade."

"My Great-Uncle Horace is the judge!"
Zoe explained.

Just then, Great-Uncle Horace's voice
boomed over the loudspeaker.

"*Hello, everybody! Happy Halloween to you
all! The costume parade is about to begin, so*

please could you all follow the path that has been lined with special silver balloons. It will take you past the zebras, the flamingos and the grizzly bears, and then finish outside the gift shop. I will be watching carefully to judge the best costume and I will announce the winner after the concert, which will come next!"

Jack looked very excited, and Nicola jumped up and down, clapping her hands and squealing eagerly. "I can't wait!" she said.

But Zoe bit her lip, suddenly feeling very nervous. She had managed to put the concert out of her mind for most of the evening, but now it was almost here, she felt more scared than ever before. She tried her best to smile at Jack and Nicola as they started walking in the costume parade, not wanting them to guess that anything was wrong.

Stephanie and Will, two of the Rescue Zoo keepers, were handing out bars of chocolate and lollies along the path, so they all helped themselves. A little bit further along, another keeper called Frankie was snapping photographs to put on the zoo's website, and called out, "You three look fantastic! Can I have a photo of you together, please?"

Jack held up his hook and growled like a pirate, while Nicola held her arms high above her head and arranged her feet like a ballerina, and Zoe put her head back and howled like a real wolf.

Suddenly Meep's ears pricked up. "Zoe, listen!" he squeaked. "Can you hear that? I think it's Shadow!"

Zoe listened and realised she *could* hear another howl over the cheery chatter of the crowd – but this one sounded very sad.

"We've got a few minutes before the concert," she whispered to Meep. "Let's see if we can slip away and go to check that he's OK. His enclosure is only round the corner." She turned to her friends. "Back in a minute!" she said to Jack and Nicola. "I just, um, forgot something I need for the concert."

"OK, Zoe. Don't be long or you'll miss it!" said Nicola.

Zoe and Meep squeezed through the crowd and ducked down an empty pathway that they knew would take them straight to Shadow. When they reached the enclosure, Zoe used her special necklace to open the gate and slip inside. As soon as the little wolf saw them, he bounded straight over to Zoe and Meep, barking happily.

"Hi, Shadow!" said Zoe, kneeling down to hug him. "I'm really sorry we couldn't stay yesterday.

What do you think of my costume?"

Shadow yapped excitedly, his little tail wagging. Zoe smiled. "Thank you! I'm glad you like it," she said. "Listen, Shadow – about your family. Don't worry about that, because today we're—"

Zoe was about to explain all about the plan to raise money for Shadow's family to come over to the zoo, but just then she heard the crackle of the loudspeaker again.

"*Wonderful costumes, everyone!*" came Great-Uncle Horace's voice. "*Now, please make your way to the green in front of the gift shop – it's time for the concert!*"

Just then, Ethan rushed down the path towards the wolf enclosure.

"Oh! Hi, Zoe!" he called, sounding surprised to see her. "Shouldn't you be over at the concert area now?"

Shadow whined curiously, wanting to know what was going on. "I'll be back as soon as I can, Shadow, I promise," Zoe whispered, then turned to smile shakily at Ethan. She rushed back down the path to join the rest of her class. This was really it!

Chapter Eight
Howling Halloween

"Zoe, there you are!" said Miss Hawkins, spotting Zoe and ushering her to her place. "We thought you were going to miss it!"

Zoe's class were standing in two lines, the people in the back line standing on a bench so that they could see. Three

microphones on stands had been set up
in front of them, like at a real concert.
As Zoe squeezed in between Nicola and
Jack, she glanced around nervously and
almost wished she *had* missed it. The zoo
was completely full, and it seemed like
thousands of people were staring right
at Zoe, even though she knew it couldn't
really be that many.

Lucy stepped up to the front, smiling
encouragingly at Zoe, and spoke into
one of the microphones. "Hello, everyone.
Welcome to the Rescue Zoo Halloween
Spooktacular, and thank you all very
much for coming. As you know, we're
raising money tonight so that we can
reunite our newest animal with his family.
We thought we would introduce you
to him, to thank you all for being so

generous already."

There was a ripple of excitement through the crowd as Ethan brought Shadow to the front and stood next to Lucy. Zoe realised that must have been why Ethan had come over to Shadow's enclosure in such a hurry.

"Oh wow, he's so cute!" Nicola said, grinning over at Zoe.

"This is Shadow, the grey wolf pup, who travelled here all the way from Alaska," Ethan announced.

Shadow gave an excited bark and a little howl, and everyone in the crowd laughed.

"Now, please give a special round of applause for Class Three from our local school, who are going to perform a Halloween song," added Lucy. "Our

zookeepers will be bringing collection
buckets round during the song, in case
you'd like to make a donation."

The crowd clapped as Miss Hawkins
started the music and Zoe's class took a
deep breath. Miss Hawkins had chosen
a couple of lines for each pair to sing by
themselves. Then they were all supposed
to join in together for the chorus.

Jenna and Sareeta started singing.

"*Spiders and slugs, creeping on the wall. . .*"
Zoe and Nicola were going to be
singing together next, and when it got
to their lines, Zoe felt her knees wobble.

"*Wild grey wolves, running through the
trees. . .*" she began very quietly, hearing
Nicola sing much more loudly next
to her.

Then she heard a little howl. Shadow
was joining in! Zoe turned and saw the
wolf pup wagging his tail happily, and
looking straight at her with bright eyes.

The crowd chuckled, and one little boy said, "They've taught the wolf how to sing along too! That's so clever!"

Zoe smiled at Shadow, and as the little pup howled happily again, she felt confident enough to sing the next line more loudly. Seeing Shadow right there reminded her why she was singing in the first place, and she really wanted to do her best. Then it was time for the whole class to sing the chorus, and Shadow burst into an even more enthusiastic howl as he heard the song get louder, and Zoe raised her voice even louder too, grinning widely.

When the song finished, the audience cheered and clapped, and some people even called for them to sing it all over again! Zoe found herself beaming, relieved it was over – but she also realised that she'd enjoyed herself. Singing wasn't so bad if you had friends to sing along with you!

Meep scampered over from where he had been perched with Lucy, watching the performance. "Zoe, you did it!" he squeaked excitedly, hopping up on to Zoe's shoulder and giving her a cuddle. "Hooray!"

Miss Hawkins stepped up to the microphone then, smiling. "Thank you! If you liked our song, please do make a donation to help us bring Shadow's pack over to the zoo."

She pointed to the collection buckets that the zookeepers were still carrying around the crowd. Zoe grinned as she saw people digging into their pockets and putting money into them. Soon they looked very full!

Ethan brought Shadow over to Zoe, and she held him carefully in her arms and gave him a hug. "Thanks for your help, Shadow," she whispered in his ear.

Shadow rubbed his furry head against Zoe's cheek and barked happily. Zoe laughed. "Howling with your pack is your favourite thing?" she said. "*Now* I understand why you've been howling so much – and why you wanted to join in with our singing!"

"Who's that?" asked Jack, nudging Zoe as someone dressed in a bright-blue bird costume stepped up to the microphone. Zoe frowned, and then started laughing as she realised who it was – and who he'd come as! "That's Great-Uncle Horace!"

she explained through a laugh. "I think he's dressed as a giant version of his pet hyacinth macaw, Kiki!"

"That was splendid! Well done to all of you!" exclaimed Great-Uncle Horace. "Now it's time to announce the prize for the best costume. This was a very hard decision, but I have picked a winner! This person will be invited to come to the Rescue Zoo and help feed our fantastic penguins!

And the winner is . . ." He paused
dramatically and then smiled.
"... the zombie ballerina over here!
Congratulations!"

Nicola's eyes almost popped out of
her head, she was so surprised. "I won!"
she gasped. "I get to come and feed the
penguins. I can't believe it!"

"Now, I have another announcement
to make!" Great-Uncle Horace continued.
"I'm delighted to say that it looks as if
we'll have raised enough money from this
evening to fly the rest of Shadow's pack
to the Rescue Zoo to be looked after here
alongside him! Thank you all for being
so generous. You are all invited back to
the zoo to meet the whole pack once
they are happily settled into their new
home!"

The audience cheered and clapped. Zoe felt a huge grin spreading over her face and cuddled Shadow even closer. "Did you hear that, Shadow?" she whispered. "Your family are coming to the Rescue Zoo! Soon you'll all be able to howl together again!"

The little wolf yapped happily and jumoed up and down excitedly.

"Now, please enjoy the rest of your evening!" said Great-Uncle Horace. "We have a home-made gingerbread stall that way. There's apple-bobbing over there. Over that way is the pin-the-tail-on-the-wolf stand! And if you would like to find out more about any of our wonderful animals, please ask one of our zookeepers, who will be delighted to help! Happy Halloween, everyone!"

"*Awoooooooooh!*"

The air was filled with howls as Zoe and Meep raced through the zoo towards Shadow's enclosure – but this time, they knew those howls didn't belong just to Shadow. It was three weeks later, and today was the day that Shadow's pack arrived at the Rescue Zoo!

Great-Uncle Horace had sent a message to Lucy using his walkie-talkie, just as Lucy and Zoe were finishing their breakfast. "The helicopter is about to land outside Shadow's enclosure! Tell Zoe to meet us there!" he'd said – so Zoe and Meep were running as fast as they possibly could!

The whole zoo had seen the helicopter circling over the zoo before it landed, and

Zoe heard animals all around her making their most friendly, welcoming noises.

"Yes, they're really here!" Zoe called happily to the excited chimpanzees, who called out to her as she passed their enclosure. "Isn't it brilliant?"

Zoe and Meep rushed around the corner just as Great-Uncle Horace and Ethan were carrying two large wooden crates into the wolf enclosure. The eager howling sound was coming from inside the crates, and Shadow was leaping all over his enclosure, barking excitedly, his tail wagging so fast it was almost a blur!

Carefully, Ethan opened the first crate, and a wolf with dark-grey markings on his side, a bit bigger than Shadow, ran out. He bounded straight over to Shadow and the two wolves nuzzled each other happily, then began to play-fight.

"That must be Shadow's big brother!" Zoe whispered to Meep.

Both wolves howled together, and then, as Ethan opened the second crate, they were joined by another wolf and two adorable babies! They nuzzled each other and made soft howling noises.

"Meep, I think I understand what *this* howling means," Zoe added. "Shadow

and his family are happy to be back together!"

"I'm happy too!" squealed Meep, bouncing up and down. "And I'm glad Shadow has his family to play with now, instead of tiny little me!"

Zoe giggled. "I can't wait to meet them all," she said. "And I can't wait to meet whatever animal Great-Uncle Horace brings home next!"

If you enjoyed Shadow's story,
look out for:

Chapter One
Summer at the Rescue Zoo!

Zoe Parker grinned as she ran out of the school gates, swinging her bag beside her. Her mum, Lucy, was waiting for her. "It's the summer holidays!" Zoe yelled, giving her mum a big hug.

Lucy smiled and ruffled her daughter's wavy brown hair. "How was the last day of term?" she asked.

Zoe began to skip excitedly along the pavement. "It was fun, but I just couldn't wait for the holidays to start. Six whole weeks!" She smiled at her mum. "And I get to spend every single day at my favourite place."

As they got closer to home Zoe heard noises ahead: roars, bellows, screeches and squeaks. Animal noises!

Finally they turned a corner, and there in front of them stood a pair of tall, beautiful gates, with a line of lush oak trees on either side. The gates were made of golden wood, and covered with delicate carvings of every sort of animal you could think of. There were majestic tigers, soaring eagles, snapping crocodiles and elegant gazelles. About halfway up, two words were carved across the gates in swirling letters: RESCUE ZOO. Right at the top, a golden hot-air balloon twinkled in the sunlight.

A queue of excited visitors were streaming through the gates, but Zoe and her mum walked straight past them.

As she stepped inside the zoo, a familiar warm, happy feeling spread through Zoe's tummy. "Home sweet home," she whispered.

Zoe and her mum weren't visiting the zoo – they *lived* there! Zoe's Great-Uncle Horace was a famous explorer and animal expert, and on his travels around the world he had met lots of animals in need of help. That was why he'd decided to build the zoo, so it could be a safe place for any creature who was lost, injured or in trouble. Now it was home to hundreds of amazing animals!

Look out for another
MAGICAL series
from Nosy Crow!

The Rescue Princesses

Look out for another AMAZING series from Nosy Crow!

Friendship, animals and secret royal adventures!